Something
about America

MARIA TESTA

CANDLEWICK PRESS

Copyright © 2005 by Maria Testa

First paperback edition 2007

The Library of Congress has cataloged the hardcover edition
as follows:

Testa, Maria.
Something about America / Maria Testa. — 1st ed.
p. cm.
ISBN 978-0-7636-2528-3 (hardcover)
1. National characteristics, American — Juvenile poetry.
2. Children of immigrants — Juvenile poetry.
3. Serbian Americans — Juvenile poetry.
4. Immigrants — Juvenile poetry.
5. Children's poetry, American.
I. Title.
PS3570.E847S66 2005
811'.54 — dc22   2005047064

ISBN 978-0-7636-3415-5 (paperback)

12 13 14 15 16 17 MVP 10 9 8 7 6 5 4 3 2

Printed in York, PA, U.S.A.

This book was typeset in Eurostile and Giovanni.

Candlewick Press
99 Dover Street
Somerville, Massachusetts 02144

visit us at www.candlewick.com

For Carlo,
all by himself

CONTENTS

MAD AT AMERICA

My father

is mad at America

and this is not

the right time,

not when American troops

are stationed

all over the world,

not when homeland security

is the most popular topic

in eighth-grade Current Events,

not when September 11 flags

are still flying

and fading,

sticking

and peeling,

everywhere.

Once,

my father loved America.

Once,

he loved life.

Once,

he loved. . . .

But he never imagined

being forced to live here

because he had

no choice,

because there was

no home anymore,

because only America

could take care

of his family.

He never imagined

being forced to live

in America

because of

me.

THREE

A memory.

I am three.
We are home
in our house
in Kosova.

I know this
not because I remember
being so young,
not because I remember
our home at all.
I know this
because I remember so well
what happened
when I was four.

A memory.

I am three.

I am sitting

on my father's lap,

playing,

patting his cheeks,

running my fingers

along his jaw line

and discovering something,

a difference.

"You have rusty cheeks!"

I announce,

and then I caress

my own face,

my own jaw line,

my own neck.

"My skin is smooth."

My father laughs

and gently pats

my cheeks.

"You are young and new

and beautiful," he says.

"And I need

a shave."

We play awhile longer,

patty-cake

clapping games,

until I curl my hand

into a fist

and bop my father

right on the nose,

surprising him

and making his eyes water,

surprising myself

that I can

surprise him.

I throw my arms

around his neck

and press my smooth cheek

against his rusty one,

an apology,

I am sorry.

My father laughs again,

louder than before.

"You are young and beautiful

and strong, too!

Ready for the world.

Look out, world!"

CUT SHORT

My family is small,

cut short

my mother says,

before we even got started.

War

has a way

of interrupting

everything.

My mother had dreams,

she says,

dreams of a university degree

and a family,

of a career in literature

and a house full of kids,

dreams of being the one

who really could

do it

all.

War

has a way

of changing

everything.

My father was happy,

my mother says,

happy to be married

and to have a daughter,

happy to work hard,

to study and struggle,

to have hope

and promise.

War

has a way

of ending

everything.

CITIZENS OF THE WORLD

We were young

when you were born,

my mother explains to me,

students looking forward

to finding our place —

strap the baby

on your back

and go

anywhere,

citizens of the world.

Life in Kosova

was all about dreams

and choices

before the war:

where to live

what to study

how to change the world.

Then the choices

changed

so suddenly,

like a flash of fire

in the sky:

where to run

where to hide

how to leave

all dreams

behind.

My mother explains it all

to me

as best she can.

We had no home anymore,

no choices —

just a burned child

who needed

America.

BECAUSE I LOOK LIKE
WHERE I'M FROM

"What's that stuff

on your neck

and on your arms?"

"What happened to you?"

"Why do you look like you do?"

My five-year-old

summer-before-kindergarten self

was not ready for the kids

in my new neighborhood

in America,

not ready for English

in all those different accents,

not ready to figure out

what I wanted to say

in any language.

I'm ready now.

I look like I do

for the same reason

I have black hair

and dark eyes

and perfect red lips.

Because I am who I am.

And because

I look like

where I'm from.

LUCKY

Lucky,

that's us,

a lucky family:

my mother

my father

and me.

Back home,

luck is measured in men,

young men

if you can find them;

how many are still

alive

in your village?

Lucky,

that's my father,

a lucky man,

not dead

not missing,

just lucky.

It does not matter

if all your possessions

were stolen

and your house was swept up

by fire

with your four-year-old daughter

trapped

inside.

It's very simple.

Lucky

means we got out

alive.

SOMETHING PRETTY SPECIAL

Now I am thirteen.

I am a typical American
schoolgirl,
happy to be in eighth grade,
and lucky to have Ms. Lee,
the best teacher
in the whole school,
because she likes us
all of us
a lot.

She knows who we are.

Our class
is a slice of America,

Ms. Lee likes to say,

and that's something

pretty special.

I do wonder sometimes

just what kind of slice

Ms. Lee has in mind.

We're nothing like

a slice of American bread

lined up neatly

with the other slices,

all wrapped

in plastic.

But we could be

a slice of pizza

with everything on it,

all the toppings mixing

together,

sometimes overpowering

one another,

sometimes spilling

out of the box.

I know we are

a slice of American style

in scarves and head coverings

and baseball caps,

we are decorated

with braids and jewelry,

we wear jeans

and silk and muslin,

we speak in slang

and accents

and silence.

In my class

I am not so different

not so unusual

not particularly unique

or exotic.

I have two languages

in my head

and no accent

on my lips

and a colorful collection

of scarves

I wear around my neck,

for fashion,

to be pretty,

my choice

my story.

IF FIRE CAN BE KIND

If fire

can be kind

then my fire

was kind

to me,

stopping

just below my chin,

stopping

just below my jaw line,

leaving

my face

untouched.

SCARVES AND MIRRORS

Hair

face

earrings

lip gloss

scarf.

Every morning,

I check out

all of them

in the mirror.

Sometimes,

I lift my scarf

slowly

so that it covers

my untouched

chin.

my untouched

lips,

my untouched

nose,

so that only

my eyes

are uncovered,

staring back at me.

Sometimes,

I wonder

about life

and being

lucky.

HOME NEVER CHANGES

Home never changes,
my father won't let it.
Even my mother
stands by him
on this one.

It's funny sometimes
how both of my parents
talk about home
as a place
with so many problems,
so behind the times,
a place
where everything needed
to change,
but still . . .
a place

with so much

promise.

Then the war started

and everything did

change,

and home

became a place

of fear

and fire

and broken promises.

So we escaped,

my mother

my father

and me.

We ran away from home.

We ran all the way

to America.

IRONY

It was easier for me

to become an American

than it was for most

of the other

refugee-immigrant-displaced kids

in my neighborhood

and at my school.

The oddest thing about me

was not my language

not my parents

not my clothes

or my religion

or my war.

No, the oddest thing about me

was that half of my skin

had been burned off,

the first thing people noticed,

the great equalizer.

I learned very quickly that

where I came from

wasn't anywhere near

as important

as what I looked like.

So it was easier for me

to become an American,

easier to be accepted as an American,

than it was for most

of the other kids

in my neighborhood

and at my school.

But it was a lot harder

for everyone

to look at me.

WHAT I LIKE ABOUT AMERICA

It's true:

I like America.

My school

my friends

my music,

everything that's important

in my life

is all-American.

And I like that America

has the best hospitals

in the world,

even my father says so

(but he doesn't exactly

look at me

when he says it).

I like the American doctors

in their clean white coats

and colorful ties

and hair ribbons

who promise me

in all kinds of accents

that things will get better,

we're learning more

every day.

And then,

most of the time,

they tell me

that I am

a normal

healthy

girl,

and beautiful.

What I like about America

best of all —

me

myself,

without asking

anyone else —

is that I think

I just might be

American.

ONE SMALL STICKER
(Like a Neon Sign)

On September 12, 2001,

my father pressed

one small sticker,

an American-flag sticker,

into a corner

of the outside window

on our front door.

He pressed it firmly,

evenly,

perfectly straight,

like it was meant

to last

forever.

It's still there.

And every time I look at it,

that one small sticker,

     fading fast

     and curling at the edges,

seems to shine as brightly

as a blinking beer sign

in a bar window.

Beer inside!

Americans inside!

Please believe us.

FOOD PROCESSING

My parents work

in food processing

for a company

that specializes

in frozen chicken

where everyone

spends the day

frying

breading

and stuffing,

and it doesn't matter

where you come from

as long as

you work hard

and don't cause trouble

and keep

your papers

in order.

Most of the adults

in my neighborhood

work for the same

company,

word of mouth

gets around

when everyone

needs a job,

when university degrees,

medical licenses,

and professional qualifications

are suddenly useless.

Sometimes at night

I lie awake in bed

and listen

to my parents

laughing their heads off

gasping for breath

about how they

never imagined

a career

in chicken.

NOT AMERICANS

My parents

are foreign,

foreigners,

immigrants,

refugees,

strangers in a strange land,

still walking around

looking like they're wondering

where someone hid

the welcome mat.

WORK IS IMPORTANT
TO A MAN

Work is important to a man,

my mother said,

and she was serious

when she told me this,

believing it

to be the truth.

Men need work

to feel whole

to feel alive

to feel like

they have a place

in the world.

And what about a woman?

I asked my mother.

What is important

to a woman?

My mother stared at me

for a moment,

noticing something,

recognizing something.

Work is important to a woman, too,

my mother said, at last.

Also important are

family and friends

neighbors and community

health and safety

peace

education

equality

love . . .

My mother was laughing,

I think,

as she left the room,

and I know

she was still talking,

adding to her list.

REALITY TV

Television gets a bad rap.

It tells a lot of lies,

I know,

but also makes everything

seem possible,

like it could even happen

to you.

I like happy endings

and I like

to watch people

with lots of huge problems

who still look beautiful

and have fun

and even laugh —

these are the shows

I like best.

My father cannot stand

American television,

cannot stand

sitcoms

police dramas

sports events

news shows

and most of all,

reality TV.

He says he's seen

nothing

on American television

that looks

anything

like the real America

he knows.

I guess he should know

what he's talking about

because he watches

American television

all

the

time.

The truth is,

television taught my father

how to speak English.

I think it's

pretty funny,

but that's

reality.

SOCCER
(Only in America)

Soccer is the most popular sport

in the world

and my father

was a pretty good player

back home,

once upon a time,

according to him.

Now he coaches

my eighth-grade team

on Tuesdays and Thursdays

after school,

and he laughs and shouts

and runs around

like he just might be having

a really good time.

But later in the day,

sitting at the dinner table

at home,

he is different:

> The greatest sport
>
> in the world
>
> is not good enough
>
> for America.
>
> Only in America
>
> is soccer
>
> a second-rate sport.
>
> Nothing
>
> is good enough
>
> for America.
>
> Nobody
>
> is good enough
>
> for America.

I know my mother

must have been

as sick and tired

of this twice-a-week speech

as I was,

she must have wanted

to tell him

to just

 shut

  up.

I knew I couldn't be

the only one

who needed

to explode:

 Why can't you say

 that you had fun?

 Why can't you say

 that you were happy?

Why can't you

just

get

over it?

So I yelled at my father.

Yeah, I know.

Only in America.

BIG FISH

My father is not a loud man,

not one to draw attention

to himself

as he goes about

his daily business.

But he's a pretty big fish

around here

in our neighborhood

where so many people

come from far away,

where so many people

are lost and confused

and a little bit scared—

to all of them,

my father is a teacher,

a leader,

a comfort . . .

a father.

A few times a month,

on a Friday or Saturday night,

a small group of men

gathers at our house

to share a bottle or two

of homemade wine,

to talk and to laugh,

to remember and to cry,

and to listen

to my father.

The group is much smaller now

than it used to be

mostly because so many

of the other men

who came here from Kosova

have gone home

with their families

now that the war is over

and there are houses,

schools, roads, and lives

to rebuild.

"A wise man, your father,"

the men will sometimes say to me,

and I know he has helped

all of them

in many important ways,

like finding jobs

and learning English,

discovering America

and, sometimes, choosing to go home.

There is no war

in Kosova

anymore.

There is a country

to rebuild,

lives to reclaim,

dreams to fulfill.

And my father remains

in America,

helping other men

decide whether or not

to go home.

MY MOTHER IS READY
TO EXPLODE

She doesn't want to have to make

any decisions,

my mother says,

because she's afraid

she's forgotten how.

Don't ask her about choices,

don't ask her what she wants—

she doesn't know anymore,

she's lost the ability

to choose,

no longer has a clue

what she wants

out of life

or even for supper tonight.

I don't believe her

when she says these things.

Somewhere,

maybe deep inside,

my mother knows

what she wants.

I know this because

she's my mother,

I'm her daughter,

and when I stare at her

I notice something,

recognize something.

My mother knows

I want to stay in America,

and she knows

my father dreams of home.

And I know

my mother is ready to explode.

SCARED

Sometimes,

when I go to bed at night

I feel a sense of panic

that I cannot explain:

Do I have a test tomorrow?

A paper due?

Did I say hello

to the wrong girl

in the hallway?

Did I lose

my favorite scarf?

Why are my parents

suddenly silent

when I enter the room?

Did we really come

all the way to America

to turn around

and go back home?

A DREAM DIVIDED

What happens to a dream divided?

A dream undefined?

A dream not agreed upon?

A dream without a name?

I envy Mr. Langston Hughes—

at least he knew what his dream

was all about

even if it was deferred,

at least he knew his dream

had the power to explode.

But what happens to a dream divided?

Does it crumble into little pieces

and get blown away by the wind,

by a whim,

scattering and landing

and taking root somewhere,

starting over?

Or does it implode?

MAD AT AMERICA
(Part 2)

My father takes everything

about America

personally,

the good and the bad,

the dreams and the reality.

Back home,

before everything changed,

he was a student of electrical engineering

and America,

and my mother remembers

how he enjoyed reciting

from memory

parts of the Declaration of Independence,

the Constitution,

the I Have a Dream speech.

America was his passion,

even before soccer,

and he wanted to bring America home,

to change the world

like a superhero,

Captain America.

Now my father

is mad at America,

mad at life,

and maybe even

mad at me.

And this is not

the right time.

LEWISTON

I had never really thought
about Lewiston before.
It was always just a city
somewhere north of here,
smaller
quieter
nowhere.

Then our television was on
even more than usual,
and the radio was on
when the television was off,
and all the adults
in the neighborhood
started talking to each other
in short, clipped
sentences.

A hate group chose Lewiston

as a place

to have a meeting,

a meeting of people

who hate people

who come from

different places,

a meeting of people

who say they love America

but hate my slice of America,

my school

my neighborhood

my mother

my father

me.

And suddenly,

Lewiston was somewhere.

CONFUSION

At first,

the news was rather funny,

an odd distraction.

It seemed

the mayor of Lewiston

wrote a letter

to the elders

of the local Somali community

saying that there were already

too many Somalis

in Lewiston

and would they please

stop sending more,

the city was "maxed out"

financially and emotionally,

and somehow,

this was the Somalis' fault.

My father laughed

at the very idea

of the mayor's letter.

"Nonsense!" he proclaimed.

"This is America, after all,

people can live

wherever they want.

There's nothing to worry about.

The mayor must be confused."

The mayor wasn't the only one.

What was the purpose of the letter?

Was it a plea?

A warning?

An invitation . . . ?

What was everyone so worried about?

And why was my father

pretending he didn't care?

MAXED OUT

Just when all of the other adults

around me

started freaking out,

my father developed

a sense of humor.

"Wow!" he exclaimed

as he sat down to dinner.

"I'm feeling quite

financially maxed out tonight."

Later in the evening

he stretched and yawned:

"I'm going to bed early—

I am physically maxed out!"

My mother shook her head

and rolled her eyes.

My father noticed.

"Your poor mother,"

he whispered to me loudly.

"I think her patience

is maxed out."

LEAFLETS

And then

some people

nobody saw

came to

our neighborhood

in the middle

of the night

and dropped

leaflets

everywhere,

all around

my school,

all around

my street,

all around

my house,

like they knew

just where

we lived.

MY PARENTS IN ACTION

My father

tore up every leaflet

he could get his hands on,

he ripped them all

into shreds,

inviting our neighbors

to join him.

Before long,

the neighborhood

was covered with tiny pieces

of confetti —

like what had happened

in the middle of the night

was some kind of

twisted block party

and not

an invasion.

My father

grabbed anyone

who would listen:

"How dare they do this

in this country?

This isn't supposed to happen

in America."

My mother

got down

on her hands and knees

in our front yard

and gathered

shreds of paper,

stuffing them into

blue trash bags.

I watched and listened to

my mother

my father

and my neighbors,

and when no one

was looking,

I read

a leaflet.

CLOSE ENOUGH

This isn't supposed to happen

in America.

In America,

people are not supposed

to say, to write, to believe

that there are too many

immigrants

dark-skinned people

Muslims

Jews . . .

People are not supposed

to say, to write, to believe

that America

is not

for everyone.

But people do.

They say it

write it

believe it

live it.

And then they come

into your neighborhood,

close enough

to drop a leaflet,

close enough

to set your house on fire.

MY FATHER ON A SCHOOL BUS

There's something
just a little strange
about sitting next to
your father
on a school bus.

It was my father's idea
to sign us up
for the rally
in the first place,
like it was some kind of
father-daughter outing,
while my mother decided
she'd rather stay home
to keep an eye

on the neighborhood

the street

the house.

"The best defense

is a good offense,"

my father said out loud

as we climbed

onto the bus,

reminding me

of his soccer

pregame speeches.

"A meeting in one part

of Lewiston

should be met with

a rally

in another part

of Lewiston.

Fear

should be met

with courage,

lies

with truth."

Everyone who heard

seemed pleased

with my father's words,

and I had to agree

that they sounded

just fine.

But I couldn't help

staring at him,

staring and smiling,

when I suddenly realized

that I had just caught

a glimpse

of Captain America.

FIRST RALLY IN THE WORLD

Our rally turned into

a party

an event

a celebration,

a gathering

of more than six thousand people,

crowding into the sports arena,

standing in the aisles,

spilling into the streets.

I sat close to my father

inside the arena

and watched him

watching everyone else,

the speakers

the singers

the dancers,

everyone from everywhere

who had the courage

to tell a story

of coming to America.

Everyone has a story.

Everyone has known

happiness and hope,

fear and sadness.

Everyone in America

is a citizen of the world.

It wasn't something

I had planned or expected,

but I felt right at home

at the rally,

like I was where

I was supposed to be,

right there with my father,

my first rally in America,

my first rally in the world.

WORD TRAVELS FAST

Word travels fast
in a crowd of six thousand people,
especially when the news
is this good:

Our rally was standing room only,
but across town
only thirty people
showed up at the meeting
that started it all,
and the best part
was that hundreds of other people
had gathered
outside that meeting
singing and chanting
so that the hate-people

wouldn't feel so good

or safe

about trying

to have a meeting

in Lewiston,

after all.

My father was impressed.

Only in America.

CONNECTION

People lingered for a while
at the end of the rally,
like they wanted it to continue,
never to end.
I trailed behind my father
as he made his way
in and out and all around
the endless rows
of folding chairs.
Then he stopped, suddenly,
reaching out his hand
to take mine,
wanting me to join him.
He led me to two people
still sitting in folding chairs,
two Somali women

in brightly colored dresses

and head coverings,

an older woman

and a younger one,

sitting alone.

My father bowed

to the women,

and I thought

of Kosova.

"My daughter," he said,

resting his hand on my shoulder.

The older woman smiled

and placed her hand

on the younger one's shoulder.

I looked at the younger woman.

She was older than me

but young enough.

I unwrapped my scarf

from around my neck.

My father bowed again.

"Welcome to America," he said.

The younger woman

leaned forward

and touched my scarf.

"Where was your war?" she asked.

LEMONADE

I've always kind of liked that saying
about making lemonade
if life gives you lemons.

Now I've got one
of my own:

If you can't find the welcome mat
when you arrive,
put one out yourself.

ALL THE WORLD'S SADNESS

My father was quiet

during the bus ride home

and that was just fine

with me.

I closed my eyes

and sat close

to him again,

enjoying the warmth

the comfort

the dreams.

Then I heard my father speak

softly

powerfully

to me:

"All the world's sadness

is in America."

I opened my eyes

to look at him.

"I know," I said,

because it was the truth.

"We all bring our sadness

to America with us."

"My sadness is here,"

my father said,

touching his chest.

Then he touched

my head

my shoulders

my heart.

"Not here."

Then he traced his finger

along my jaw line

along my arms

along my scars.

"Not here."

A memory. I am three.

"Rusty cheeks," I said softly.
"I remember rusty cheeks."

I watched my father's face crash
but he did not look away,
and I loved him.

"You are young and beautiful
and strong," my father said.
"Ready for the world."

LOVE POEM FOR MY FATHER

I will hold your heart

in both of my hands

for as long

as you will let me.

It would be nice

if you would hold mine too,

but it's okay

if you have to let go,

I'll be just fine.

I am ready

to make my heart whole

all by myself.

Also by Maria Testa

Becoming Joe DiMaggio

**An American Library Association
Notable Children's Book**

**An International Reading Association
Children's Choice**

**A New York Public Library
100 Titles for Reading and Sharing Selection**

★ "Powerfully moving as it braids together
baseball, family, and the Italian-American
experience." —*Booklist* (starred review)

★ "A powerful, glowing, unforgettable
achievement."
—*Kirkus Reviews* (starred review)

Available in paperback

With a father at war, a year can seem like forever.

Almost Forever
by Maria Testa

A Book Sense 76 Selection

**A New York Public Library
100 Titles for Reading and Sharing Selection**

A Chicago Public Library Best Book

★ "Rapt readers don't need to know anything
   about Vietnam to understand love, loss,
   fear, and waiting. A tour de force."
   — *Kirkus Reviews* (starred review)

"A testament to spouses and children left
stateside. . . . Don't expect to make it
through with dry eyes."
— *Bulletin of the Center for Children's Books*

Available in paperback